A Pony for the Winter

By HELEN KAY

Pictures by INGRID FETZ

SCHOLASTIC BOOK SERVICES

NEW YORK · TORONTO · LONDON · AUCKLAND · SYDNEY

FOR DEBBIE
who always wanted a horse, so Joanie could ride.

This edition has been especially edited for Lucky Book Club readers.

Copyright © 1959, 1964 by Helen Kay and Ingrid Fetz. This edition is published by Scholastic Book Services, a division of Scholastic Magazines, Inc., by arrangement with Farrar, Straus & Co., Inc.

26 25 24 23 22 21 20 19 18   7 8 9/7 01/8
Printed in the U.S.A.

07

CONTENTS

Deborah's Wish

One bright September day ponies began to appear at the foot of Nannyhagen Road — lots of them. Deborah could see them from the school bus in the morning, their tails swishing this way and that. And she could see them from the school bus in the afternoon, their tails swishing that way and this.

At home she asked, "Why can't I have a pony?"

"Ponies are work," Dad explained. And he went on reading his newspaper. "Get a turtle. Turtles are small and no work at all."

A turtle was too tame even to think about. "I would work for my pony," Deborah begged.

Dad did not answer, but Mother patted Deborah's head. She understood.

"A pony would be nice," said big brother Lewis.

Little sister Joan took out her cowboy boots and began to polish them. "I'll ride Deborah's pony," she said.

But how was Deborah to get a pony?

She picked up Dad's paper, and she saw an advertisement: "Horses. Just the right pet for your child. Trained for saddle and cart. Cheap. Pleasantville 5-9980."

Deborah went quietly to the telephone in

the hallway, dialed the number, and asked in the most grown-up voice she could manage, "How much is your horse?"

"Two hundred and fifty dollars," a man's voice answered.

Deborah hung up the phone softly. Two hundred and fifty dollars! How could she ever get a horse — or even a pony? Deborah went slowly up to bed. She hugged her pillow sadly, as though it were a pony's neck. Ponies were big dreams and far, far away.

A Pony Ride

The dreams were far away, but the ponies were right there at the foot of the hill. And Saturday morning Deborah went down to get a closer look. There she saw the ponies — tan and white, sorrel and brown, and one very small black one.

Deborah watched in wonder. "Just my size," she said to herself. She watched the man working with the small black pony.

"Like ponies?" The man smiled at Deborah. "Want a ride?"

"Me?" Deborah cried. "Oh yes!" She climbed the fence and jumped into the corral.

Strong arms lifted her high in the saddle. She held the reins. The world was hers. Everything looked different from the pony's back — the ground so far below and the sky so close above. She felt very tall on the pony's back.

She rode slowly around the field. When the pony reached the post again, Deborah got down and asked shyly, "Can I come again?"

"We won't be here much longer. All the ponies are going," the man said.

"Are you giving them away?" Deborah began to hope. Maybe he would give one to her!

"These are the ponies from Playland Park," the man said. "They work hard all summer long. In the winter we board them out. We've got just one that isn't spoken for."

Deborah could hardly say thanks and goodbye fast enough. She ran all the way up the hill. And she didn't stop running until she found Mother in the kitchen.

A Pony for the Winter

Deborah was puffing and panting. The words came tumbling out too fast to make sense. But somehow Deborah made Mother understand. *There was a pony who needed a home!*

"So you want to board a pony for the winter," Mother said. "You know that means work."

"But Mother, I know. I'll work, I promise," Deborah begged. A lump stuck in her throat, and the words were bottled up inside.

"It will mean work for all of us, Deborah,"
Mother said.

Deborah held onto Mother's hand tightly.

"You mean you can get this pony for free?"
Lewis asked. He was impressed. "Let her have
it, Mom."

"It will mean work for you too, Lewis," Mother said. "We'll all have to help Deborah. Are you sure you'll want to?"

"Say yes, Lewis, say yes," Deborah begged.

"Sure," Lewis promised. "I'll carry the water. But don't forget, I won't do everything."

"I'll help too," said Joan. "I'll give it sugar lumps."

At last Mother agreed to talk to the man. But it was understood that Dad would have the last word. Soon they were all driving down the hill.

The man was still there. "Have you come for a pony?" he asked Mother, smiling. "I'm Mr. Carter."

"Well," said Mother, laughing, "I'm not sure. Tell me about these ponies."

Deborah held her breath. Would she get the pony? Why did they *have* to talk so much?

"I run the pony rides at Playland," Mr. Carter was saying. "For ten cents any child can ride my ponies. Every day it's ponies and children,

children and ponies, up and down, around and around. So when the summer is over, I go far away from ponies and children. I go fishing in Florida."

While Mr. Carter was talking, they went through a gate into the corral. "Which pony will be mine?" Deborah wondered.

"I understand you have one last pony left," Mother was saying.

"Just one more, and that's Mollie, over there," Mr. Carter pointed to the little black pony, the very one Deborah had ridden.

"Will she be good with little children?" Mother asked. "Deborah is only eight, and Joan is four."

"Mollie'll be all right. But she does pin her ears back," Mr. Carter warned.

"What does that mean?" Mother asked.

"Stubborn, just stubborn," explained Mr.

Carter. And as he passed Mollie, he gave her a playful slap.

Deborah looked at Mollie's ears. They stood up straight, as all good pony ears should.

"A coffee can full of oats in the morning is all she needs, and an armful of hay at night. Plenty of water, though. I'll bring her up next Saturday around noon," Mr. Carter said.

Deborah could hardly believe it. The pony was coming! She held onto the fence tightly to keep from flying away with joy.

Mother warned her: "Remember, this is a borrowed pony, Deborah. Will you be able to give it back next spring?"

"Oh yes!" Deborah said. She would have said almost anything to get that pony.

But to herself she wondered, "Will I?" But now it was September, and spring was far, far away. Why worry about spring? All she could think was, "I have a pony — now, now, now!" and everything inside of her seemed to be galloping.

A Pony Named Mollie

Next Saturday everyone was in the barn, busy building a stall for Mollie. Lewis helped with hammer and nails. Joan had an apple ready. Deborah had a box of sugar.

Father warned, "Be careful. Don't let Mollie nip your fingers when you feed her."

Deborah held out her palm with the sugar lump in it.

"That's the way. And I hope you understand, too," Dad said, "that Mollie is only borrowed?" He hammered more nails into the pony stall. "When the time is up, you will have to give her back."

"I know," said Deborah, "but she's my pony for the winter."

It took a long time to fix up Mollie's stall. One o'clock came and went, and still no pony. Deborah laid an extra-high pile of straw at one end of the stall. It would make a good bed.

"When is that pony coming?" Deborah asked Dad. "Maybe Mr. Carter forgot about us. Maybe he isn't going to bring her!"

"Deborah, get the water buckets," Dad said. He kept everyone busy putting the barn in order. "Lewis, you fill the buckets with water." An old tub was to be Mollie's drinking trough.

At last Deborah heard the pony truck in the driveway.

"Here we are!" Mr. Carter shouted, and he jumped out. Now he was backing Mollie down the ramp. As soon as the pony was on the ground, she began to eat the grass.

Deborah was speechless. "My very own pony," she whispered. Mollie was everything a little pony should be. Her mane was full, her tail was long, and on her black nose was a pretty white mark. Not exactly a star, Deborah decided, but a beauty spot. Deborah threw her arms around Mollie, but Mollie just went on eating the grass.

"How old is she?" Deborah asked Mr. Carter.

"Eight years old," was the reply.

"Just my age!" thought Deborah. And she felt this was a sign that Mollie belonged to her.

Just then Mollie lifted her head. She looked them all over quickly. Then she went back to the grass again. She gathered a mouthful with a crunch, crunch, crunch, and chewed it slowly with a munch, munch, munch. Deborah's heart leaped. She knew Mollie had looked longest at her.

Mr. Carter showed Dad how to put the bit into Mollie's mouth, how to fasten the belts to the saddle under her belly, and how to adjust the stirrups. Deborah listened carefully as Mr. Carter told them what to do. "Ponies are tough," he explained. "Let her graze in the field. Curry her with a scrub brush, but not too often. She'll grow a coat of hair like a bear, to keep warm. She'll be fine." Mr. Carter gave Dad a contract which read: "I agree to board this pony until the month of April, and to give her veterinary care in case of need."

As Mr. Carter drove off, Deborah led Mollie into the clean new stall. The pony lay right down on the straw bed and rolled over. She snorted with pleasure. Deborah hung onto the gate and smiled. She knew Mollie liked it here.

"Two rules," Dad said. "No one rides Mollie without a grownup around. And no one gets behind her where she can kick."

Deborah looked surprised. Mollie kick? That soft, cuddly, toy pony kick her? Deborah smiled knowingly to herself.

Ponies Are a Lot of Fun

Mollie came to the Browns in September. She was to stay for eight months. That was a long time, Deborah thought happily. And she prepared to enjoy herself.

The first thing she did was to change her hair style to a pony tail. She tied it with a ribbon —bright red. Her hair hung down long and silky, and she could toss it about.

The next day, before breakfast, all three children went outside to feed Mollie. Lewis carried two big buckets of water, Deborah carried almost a pailful, and Joan carried a glassful. Mollie was watered.

Then Lewis began to groom the pony with his brush. Joan washed the pony's soft velvet nose, while Deborah worked on her mane and forelock. She tied a big bow to Mollie's mane — bright red like her own. Mollie snorted with happiness. It was plain that she was glad to be getting so much attention.

First the children gave Mollie a pail of oats. Then they went inside to eat their own sausages and griddle cakes. Soon after breakfast the lawn looked like a school playground. Children were everywhere. How had they heard? It was as though bells were ringing and singing, "Pony rides! Free pony rides!"

"Saddle her up," Dad said to Lewis.

"Can't I saddle her?" Deborah asked her father.

"When you've learned how," Dad promised.

Deborah held Mollie by the lead rope. Lewis put the bit into her mouth. Then he pulled the reins over her head. Next, he threw the saddle over her back and strapped it under her belly. He made the stirrups shorter. Deborah was to get the first ride, and Dad helped her up.

"Why, I'm even taller than Dad," Deborah thought as she sat on her pony. Deborah pulled the left rein when she wanted to go left. She pulled the right rein when she wanted the pony to go right. She pulled both reins tight together when she wanted Mollie to stop.

Mollie would give a little snort and then look at Deborah sideways. It was just as if the pony were saying, "How do you like me?"

"I love you!" Deborah answered. Then she rode back to the others. She was ready to give someone else a turn.

Now Lewis made the stirrups longer for himself, but they couldn't be let out far enough for his long legs. Lewis began to sing "Get along,

little dogie," and everyone laughed as he rode with his legs almost touching the ground.

Lewis was too big for Mollie. He looked like a big boy riding a little tricycle. "Mollie is really mine," said Deborah to herself, and she felt good.

Next, Dad let Deborah make the stirrups shorter for Joan. Deborah felt as though she'd been buckling straps all her life.

Dad lifted Joan into the saddle and gave

Deborah the lead rope. Deborah felt very important as she led the pony around the field.

In the meantime children lined up according to size, with the littlest first. Deborah waited while Dad gave everyone a ride. It took a long time. Dad and the pony were both tired. They were both walking with their heads down. Every time Dad thought he was finished, another child had to have a turn.

Finally Dad gave up. "I'm tired, and Mollie's tired," he said. "From now on there'll be rides only on Sunday afternoons."

Deborah led Mollie back to the barn.

How long would it be before she could saddle Mollie up and take her out all by herself?

Deborah put ribbons on Mollie to see where they would look best — on her tail, or on her mane, or on her forelock. After all, Mollie was a girl, wasn't she?

Ponies Are a Lot of Work

Those September and October days were times to remember.

Deborah's feet would make the leaves crunch as she came near Mollie. Mollie's ears would prick up. Mollie was learning that Deborah brought good things. Sometimes it was a sugar lump, sometimes it was an apple.

Deborah was learning, too. She could now saddle Mollie all by herself. Soon Dad said she could ride Mollie alone into the field. After each ride Deborah enjoyed taking care of Mollie. Everyone helped.

Even Joan helped clean the stall. The manure was piled in a heap. They would use it in the spring on the strawberry plants.

Joan was the first to get tired of taking care of Mollie. After all, she was only four years old. Then Lewis began to complain. His friends had to wait for him while he finished helping Deborah. "It's really your pony," he said.

It was true. Joan was too little, and Lewis was too big for the pony. Deborah would have to try to do more herself.

When the children lined up for rides outside the barn door, Deborah had an idea. "You want a ride?" she asked. "Good. Then help me clean up!" That way Lewis could go play ball and there would still be helpers. Or so Deborah thought.

Next day no one came to ride. No one wanted to help with the work. So Deborah had to face it alone.

Mollie was out in the meadow. She was rolling in the clover and kicking her feet high in the air. Deborah wished she could go for a ride. But first the stall had to be cleaned. She put out fresh straw for Mollie to lie on. Then she brought in hay for the night.

Mother sent Lewis out with water. "I did promise to carry the water," he said. He looked a little guilty as he went off to play ball.

Now Deborah was alone in the barn, working. "Ponies *are* a lot of work," she said to herself.

Resting on her shovel, Deborah looked through the barn door. She could see Mollie eating apples under a tree. First Mollie ate all that lay on the ground. Then she began to eat the apples on the tree.

When the lower branches became bare, Deborah watched Mollie stand up on her hind legs and reach for apples on the higher branches. Deborah laughed. "Mollie, are you trying to climb the tree?"

Still smiling, she turned back to work when something else caught her eye.

A girl in jeans was coming across the field. She was coming closer and closer. The girl stopped near Mollie to pet and talk to her, and Deborah saw that it was her friend, Katie.

Katie had walked two miles from the village to see Deborah and her pony. "I just love

horses," she said. "I'll clean the stall or do anything for a ride, Debbie."

Deborah was so glad to have a helper, she wanted to hug Katie. The two girls worked quickly and quietly together. And soon the stall was clean as a whistle.

Then Deborah caught and saddled Mollie. She helped Katie get on the pony and led her around the field.

"What are you going to do when Mollie goes?" Katie asked.

"I'll figure out some way to keep her," Deborah said.

Mollie Loves Deborah

Later, after Katie had gone home, Deborah began to wonder how she could keep her pony. Deborah knew the pony had come to love her. Mollie was always waiting for her near the fence post where the school bus stopped. And while Deborah changed her clothes, Mollie galloped about impatiently. That was another sign Mollie loved her.

Every day Deborah would put on her jeans and go to Mollie's stall to get all the work done. Once, while she was bending over to rake the stall clean, she felt a nibble at her back. Mollie had come in out of the field to kiss her.

"Shoo," Deborah shouted. "I'll be out soon." But Mollie did not want to go away. She ran out of the barn and then came back again, teasing.

"What do you want?" Deborah asked. "You want me to ride you?"

Deborah put up the rake and saddled Mollie. Sitting on her pony, Deborah had suddenly grown tall as tall. This was the magic of riding. It gave one size. It gave one wings. Deborah felt a glow inside as she rode out of the corral, across the field, and through the woods. The leaves of the trees brushed against her cheek. Her head was touching the sky.

In the open spaces Mollie picked up speed, and Deborah felt the wind on her face. In the wooded places Mollie slowed down, and Deborah ducked her head to keep the branches from scratching her.

Bending low over her pony, she whispered, "I love you, Mollie." Mollie's sides were smooth as velvet, and her rough mane felt good to

Deborah's fingers. And as for her steamy smell — Deborah thought it was the best smell in the whole world. She could see Mollie's pretty ears quivering, and Deborah knew this meant, "I love you, Deborah."

Back at the barn, Debbie took off Mollie's saddle, wiped her dry, and sent her off to feed in the meadow. Then, cheerfully, Deborah went back to her chores.

All through the Indian summer, Katie came to help Deborah. It was a nice walk up the hill from the village when a pony ride waited at the other end. But when it started to rain — cold, wet, sleety rain — Katie couldn't walk up the hill any more.

One day she telephoned Deborah. "Let's hide Mollie at my house," she said. "Then no one will know where she is, and she won't have to go back to Playland."

"Oh no," Debbie said. "We couldn't do that."
But the idea stayed.

A Long Winter

Deborah had all the chores to do. Now there was no one to help her. Joan was too small; Mother was too busy; Dad was away at work; the children didn't come to ride, now that they knew ponies were work. There was only Lewis, her big brother. She'd have to ask him.

"Lewis, please —" she began.

"I know, I know. You need help with Mollie. But I only said I'd carry the water. I've got homework and I'm busy," he said.

Deborah kept her fist folded tight. She had something in it. "I'll give you all my money, every bit, if you'll just help me through this bad weather," she begged. And she held out all of her ten dollars to Lewis.

"Keep it," Lewis grumbled, his face turned red. "I'll help." And they went out and worked in the cold. Mollie gave off friendly, steamy snorts — to warm them, Deborah was sure.

The next morning it rained even more. Lewis was late for his school bus, and he hurried with his buckets. He was getting wet from the rain, and wetter still from the water sloshing over on his pants. He had to rush upstairs to change into dry clothes.

"Hold the bus for me!" he called. He was angry at having to dress twice for school.

As he ran for the bus, the door slamming after him, he shouted, "Why did we ever get that pony?"

To save time, they put the water buckets out the night before. In the morning the water was frozen solid outside the kitchen door. The school bus was waiting. Now Lewis gave up. "Mother," he called, "you'll have to water Mollie." And he was gone.

"I'll carry the buckets," Deborah said. Her bus came later. "I'm big enough." Suddenly she felt much bigger. Mollie was her pony, after all. So Deborah thawed out the water pails in the downstairs bathroom.

But she could only fill them a quarter full, and Deborah's arms grew tired from carrying the buckets back and forth. Mollie would take one long drink of water, and the trough would be empty. And all the while she complained with little snorts and sighs. "You're awfully slow. And why so late this morning?" she seemed to say.

Mollie was prepared for winter, if no one else was. Her coat was a thick glossy black. It shone like velvet. Her mane and her tail were bushy and beautiful.

"My Mollie," Deborah sighed. And she rubbed her cold, chapped little hands against Mollie's plump velvet sides. Mollie answered her with a friendly whinny. Mollie's soft coat warmed Deborah's hands. And the three long hairs on Mollie's nose tickled Deborah's nose when Mollie kissed her. And Deborah's heart was full of Mollie.

"Ponies are a lot of work," Deborah scolded.

Then she threw her arms around Mollie's neck and cried, "But you're worth it!"

When the first snow began to fall, Deborah let Mollie out to play. The pony frisked about making hoofmarks in the soft white stuff. She jumped and leaped and ran around and around. Mollie was as happy as a puppy. She even ate the snow.

"Can we ride her, Mother?" Deborah asked.

"No dear, I think you'd better not. She might slip and fall without snowshoes," Mother said, and she went back into the warm house.

"Let's put galoshes on her," said Joan.

It seemed a good idea. Out came two pairs of galoshes, and while Joan fed Mollie wisps of hay, Deborah buckled the boots onto Mollie's four feet. When she was sure that Mollie couldn't slip, she hitched her sled to Mollie's harness. Now they were ready for snow fun.

Somehow Mollie didn't seem to agree. She stood very still. Deborah and Joan sat on the sled waiting. What was happening to Mollie's

ears? They were folding back to the sides of her head! "Come on, Mollie," Deborah urged. "Gidyap!" shouted Joan.

Mollie moved, but not to walk. She yanked herself free of the sled, and into the snow flew Deborah and Joan. Galloping wildly, tossing galoshes this way and that, Mollie showed them that she did not like to pull sleds. Then she rolled over and over in the snow, trying to get rid of the reins and rope.

Deborah helped Joan out of the snow and brushed her off. Joan went into the house crying. "I don't care if Mollie goes!" she called back. "I'd rather have a parakeet anyway!"

Deborah ran to Mollie. But her pony's ears were still down. "So that's what Mr. Carter meant by pinning her ears back," thought Deborah.

She took a sugar lump out of her pocket. Mollie's ears perked up again, the way all good pony ears should. Deborah led her back into the barn and pulled off the last of the galoshes and the reins and the rope. She wanted to make up with Mollie somehow. She ran upstairs for her own blanket. "It might get awfully cold," she said to Mollie as she put the blanket over the pony's back.

But Mother was right behind her. "This is a pony, not a horse," she said. "Mollie has a thick coat to keep her warm, and *you'll* need your blanket tonight. I'll take it back up now. And isn't it almost time for Mollie's dinner?"

Mollie snorted. When Deborah piled the hay high for an extra-big feed, the pony gave her a kiss as though to say, "I understand."

The snow stayed on the ground, thick and hard. Ice formed on top of it. It was cold weather even for ponies. Weeks went by, and the snow and ice and sleet kept Mollie in the barn. She grew fat and lazy from lack of exercise. But she still had to be fed.

Deborah carried water until her arms seemed to be falling off. The water was always freezing over. It froze over in the trough and in the pails and on the path to the barn. But the snow and ice melted at last. The cold rains gave way to warm ones. And one bright day Mollie was out again.

Winter Is Over!

The snow was gone and the sun was out — it was a good day for riding.

But Mollie had ideas of her own. She had been locked up in that stall for weeks. Now that she was finally out, she wanted to be free. She leaped through the air like an acrobat. She rolled in the mud. When she got up, she looked like a mud ball. It would take all day

to clean her up — if she could be caught. Mollie
had found a new plaything — the lovely mud
of springtime.

As for riding, if anyone so much as touched
the saddle, Mollie would pin her ears back and
grind her front hooves into the ground. Deborah
was the only one who could come close to her.
Maybe Mollie was mean and sassy, but she still
loved Deborah.

"Mr. Carter will be back any day," Dad said. He sounded almost glad that Mollie would be going, Deborah thought.

Joan was trying to decide if she wanted a pussycat or a parakeet to take Mollie's place. Lewis got out his mitt and ball, and started warming up for spring practice. But Katie came back to help.

Katie's Plan

There was no more riding. "She's had a hard winter," Deborah explained to Katie. "That's why we can't ride her."

Katie was helping Deborah groom Mollie. "We could still take her down to my house," whispered Katie.

Deborah knew that, with good weather, Mollie would get back into shape. If she could only keep her always! Maybe Katie was right,

Deborah thought to herself, and she began to brush Mollie harder than ever. If Mollie couldn't be the riding-est pony, at least she'd be the shining-est. And shine Mollie did, like a black-velvet toy.

April first came and went, and no Mr. Carter.

"Gee," Lewis cried. "Maybe he won't come back, and we'll be stuck with Mollie."

"Hurray! Hurray!" shouted Deborah. "She'll be mine forever!"

But she knew that sooner or later Mr. Carter would come back for Mollie. She said so to Katie, and Katie had a plan.

"Why don't we lead her down the road to my house? Then when the man comes, he won't know where she is. And when he goes away, you can come and visit Mollie."

"But she's a borrowed pony," Deborah said. Then she stopped. Wasn't Mollie really hers? She had cleaned and curried her, fed and watered her. She had talked and whispered to her. And Mollie had told Deborah a hundred secrets, too.

"Let's go," Katie said, "or you'll never see her again."

That did it. Deborah thought of how she had worked for Mollie. And she remembered how Mollie would wait for her at the gate. No. Mollie *couldn't* go away.

The girls decided that Mollie should go to Katie's house right away. Deborah gave Katie the lead rope and opened the gate, and Katie began to go down the hill to the village. They began well enough. But Mollie had a mind of her own, and she wasn't used to being led. With one yank she broke her neckpiece. Then she turned about and galloped back up the hill, tail and mane flying. And Katie was left holding the harness.

The minute Katie had disappeared down the road, Deborah began to worry.

The pony was for the children at Playland. She belonged to Mr. Carter. He had lent Mollie to her for the winter to take care of. And here she was going back on her bargain! She *had* to catch up with Katie and bring Mollie back.

Just as Deborah was running downhill, the pony was running up. Deborah reached out to grab her halter, but all she got was a long hair from Mollie's mane. There was nothing to grab hold of.

"Mollie!" she called. Mollie slowed for a moment and then galloped on.

Deborah called again, but Mollie was teasing now. She galloped faster than ever.

Then Deborah had an idea. She ran into the barn and put some oats in the feed dish. Mollie saw it and came back at a gallop, glad to get her favorite food. Deborah slammed the gate shut behind her. Mollie was safely home. Now she'd be ready to go back to Playland with Mr. Carter.

Breathless and teary, Katie appeared with the broken harness in her hand.

"We just can't do it," Deborah explained. "It isn't right." And Katie nodded her head. Both girls knew it would have been wrong.

Deborah put her arm around Katie, and walked sadly to Mother with the broken harness. All Mother said was, "I think we can get it fixed at the shoemaker's." Deborah wondered if Mother knew more than she let on.

Good-bye to Mollie

On the last Saturday of April, Deborah was in the stall with Mollie when she heard a sound in the driveway. Her heart sank. It was the pony truck, and out stepped Mr. Carter.

There was no hope now. It was really time for Mollie to go. Deborah threw her arms around Mollie, and a tear rolled down her

cheek. Yes, Mollie had been lots of work, but ponies were such good company. Mollie's soft nose nuzzled against Deborah's cheek.

Deborah could see Mother coming out of the house to talk to Mr. Carter. Then she saw them both coming toward her. She kept her face hidden in the pony's mane, so they wouldn't see tears in her eyes.

Mr. Carter looked Mollie over.

"She's fat enough," he said. "But you've been too easy on her."

He took Mollie's lead rope, but Mollie would not budge. He gave her a whack on the back, but still the pony stood beside Deborah.

"Will she pin her ears back?" Deborah wondered.

Mr. Carter picked up a stick.

"Don't hit her!" Deborah cried, "I'll help." Even though she hated doing it, she led Mollie up the ramp of the truck. Then she petted her and came down again. Mollie stayed.

"Say, that pony likes you," Mr. Carter said.

But Deborah was too miserable to answer. It was all she could do to manage a weak smile.

"Want her for next year?" Mr. Carter asked as he was ready to drive off.

Suddenly the smile became a real one, and tears of happiness filled Deborah's eyes. "Oh yes, oh yes!" she shouted, dancing up and down the road.

Mother opened her mouth to say "No." But she looked at Deborah, and Deborah knew that

Mother had to say "Yes." Now it was different. Now Deborah knew how to take care of Mollie. Now they belonged to each other. She was only lending Mollie back for the summer. Deborah felt big and generous. It was almost easy to part with Mollie now that it was only for a short time.

After Mr. Carter had gone, Deborah and Mother turned to the empty barn.

"Are you sure you want Mollie back next year?" Mother asked Deborah. "Don't forget, you'll have to clean and curry her, water and feed her, all winter long."

"Oh yes," Deborah answered right away. "Mollie's mine now."

Mollie and Debbie Meet Again

Soon after the summer holiday began, Katie invited Debbie to go with her to Playland Park.

The girls rushed through the whole park to
the pony corral. There they were, tails swishing

this way and that, sorrel and brown, white and gray. And yes, one small black pony was standing near the fence — a small black pony with a little white mark on the nose.

"There she is!" shouted Katie. "There's Mollie."

Debbie ran to the rail. She got out a lump of sugar and held it out to Mollie. The little pony lifted herself up on her hind legs and gave a joyful snort. Yes, Mollie remembered!

"Hey! that pony knows you!" said a boy who had been watching Deborah and Mollie.

"Yes," said Deborah. "Her name is Mollie, and she is my pony for the winter. I'm lending her to Playland Park for the summer."

And Deborah thought of the time when she would again sit on Mollie, brushing the leaves of the trees as she rode by, tall as tall, head touching the sky.

And the work? Of course, Deborah knew, ponies were lots of work.

Some other books by Helen Kay:
A Duck for Keeps*
A Summer to Share
The Magic Mitt

*Available from Scholastic Book Services